This igloo book belongs to:

....

igloobooks

Published in 2015
by Igloo Books Ltd
Cottage Farm
Sywell
NN6 0BJ
www.igloobooks.com

LEO002 0515
4 6 8 10 9 7 5
ISBN 978-1-78343-652-1

Written by Melanie Joyce
Illustrated by Maurizia Rubino

Printed and manufactured in China

Melanie Joyce • Maurizia Rubino

Big Bad Bunny

igloobooks

Beyond the wild-flower meadow,
in Cherry Blossom Wood,
the animals lived quietly
in their leafy neighbourhood.

Life was simply perfect and
things were always the same.
Until one day a **stranger** arrived...

Big Bunny was his name.

Big Bunny came bouncing by.
"I'm moving in here," he said.

He dug an enormous burrow and flicked soil overhead.

He thumped his back foot crossly and dived down, underground.

"What are **YOU** all staring at?" boomed Big Bunny, looking around.

"Maybe he's just **shy**," said Owl.
"It's not easy when you're new.
Make Big Bunny welcome and
he'll soon make friends with you."

So, the field mice invited him to come for tea at four.

They heard him bounding down the path...

... and **thump** on their front door.

Big Bunny had terrible manners.
He gobbled up all the food.

He **chomped** on the cake
and **slurped** the cream.
He was really very rude.

"Come swimming with us," said the otters. "You'll think it's really cool."

"Alright," said Big Bunny, giggling, but then...

... he **farted** in the pool.

When the baby badgers were napping,
Big Bunny shouted...

"BOO!"

"You naughty bunny," they squealed.
"We've **had enough** of you!"

The animals of Cherry Blossom Wood
were cross and a little bit sad.
"We've tried our best," they said to Owl,
"but that Big Bunny is just so BAD!"

Owl sat and thought for a while.
"I've got a plan," he said.
"We won't be mean to Bunny.
We'll do something **nice** instead."

Owl whispered to the animals
and everyone seemed delighted.

They began to run all over the wood
and were terribly **excited**.

The squirrels gathered nuts and the mice found lovely treats.

The badgers blew up balloons and the otters made some sweets.

In their den the little foxes all began to bake.

"There's no time to lose," they said.
"There are **lots** of things to make."

The smells in Cherry Blossom Wood
were sugary and delicious.
Big Bunny got a **whiff**
and soon became suspicious.

"Something's up," he thought.
"I definitely smell a rat.
"They're having fun **without me.**
I'll put an end to that."

He bounded into the clearing...

... and hopped with one great **LEAP**.

"Ah-ha!" he cried, bouncing off the jelly and landing in a heap.

Big Bunny felt a bit silly,
as everyone stood and stared.
"This is all for **YOU**," said Owl.
"We wanted to show you we cared."

"I'm sorry," said Big Bunny. He suddenly felt so sad.
"Cheer up!" cried the other animals. "You're really not **that** bad."

"Let's get the party started!" cried Owl.
"We'll make Big Bunny **welcome** here."
"Yes, please!" cried Big Bunny, bouncing,
as everyone gave a cheer.

Big Bunny was never bad after that, because he had **lots** of friends.

Cherry Blossom Wood was **perfect** again and that is how the story ends!